Hedgehugs
Hide and Squeak

For Connor Bear,
love and hope and
HedgeHUGS always.
#ChasingConnorsCure

Horace and Hattie are the very best of friends.

There are so many things they like to do together.

They like to make funny shadows as the sun comes up.

They like to follow shiny snail trails,

and catch the drips from leaves.

And early in the morning, they like
to spot the sparkling spider webs.

When Horace is busy, Hattie likes to decorate her nest with pretty things.

When Hattie is busy, Horace likes to practise his music.

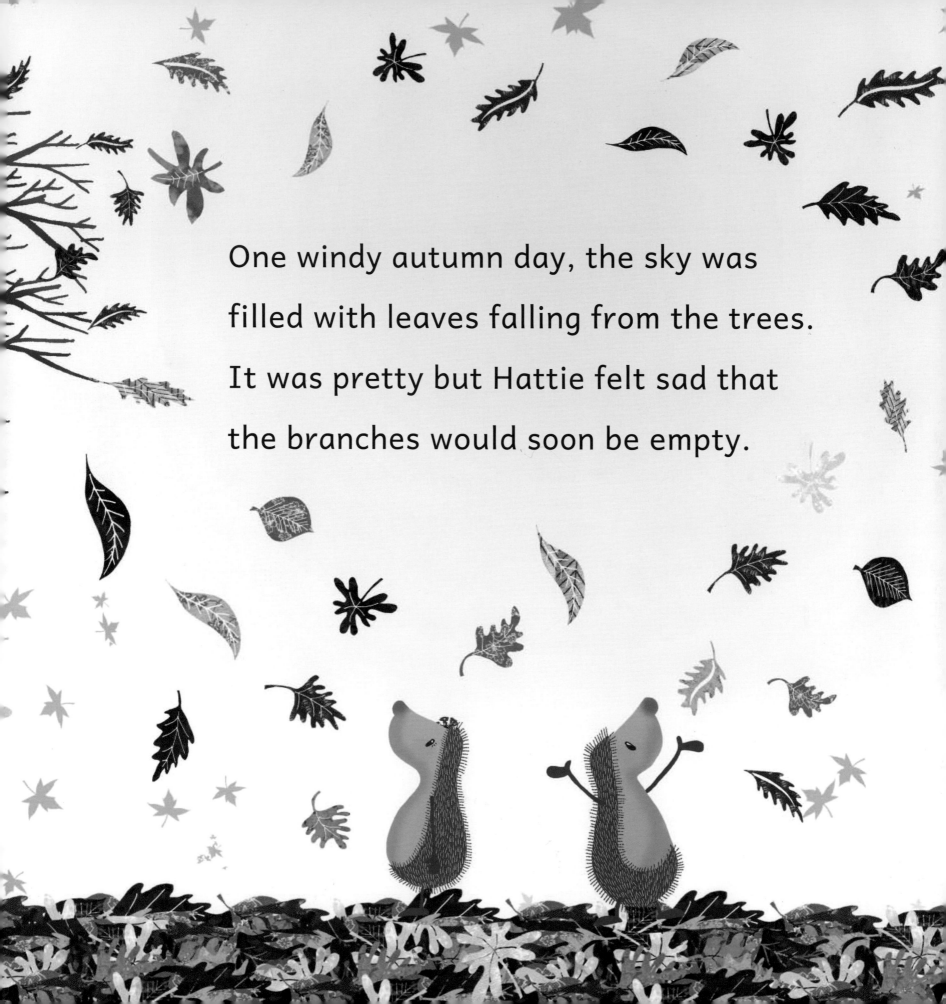

One windy autumn day, the sky was filled with leaves falling from the trees. It was pretty but Hattie felt sad that the branches would soon be empty.

Horace didn't like Hattie to be sad so he gathered up all the best and brightest leaves.

He reached up to hang
them back on a branch.

Suddenly
something
squeaked!

Horace and Hattie leapt with surprise
and landed in a large leafy pile.

The squeaky thing thought it was a game –
he loved to play hide and seek!

Horace and Hattie loved to play
games too; they were experts
at hiding...

...and seeking. First Horace and Hattie searched for their new friend in the blackberry bushes.

When they found him hidden in a tangle of brambles, he squeaked with joy.

It took the squeaky thing ages to spot his prickly friends

amongst the spiky seed pods.

Horace and Hattie knew the squeaky thing was hidden somewhere beneath the toadstools and mushrooms.

'Squeak!' At last they
found him in the fungus!

The three friends giggled.

It was so much fun playing 'hide and squeak'!

But Horace had one last hiding place

– he'd spied a splendidly secret spot...

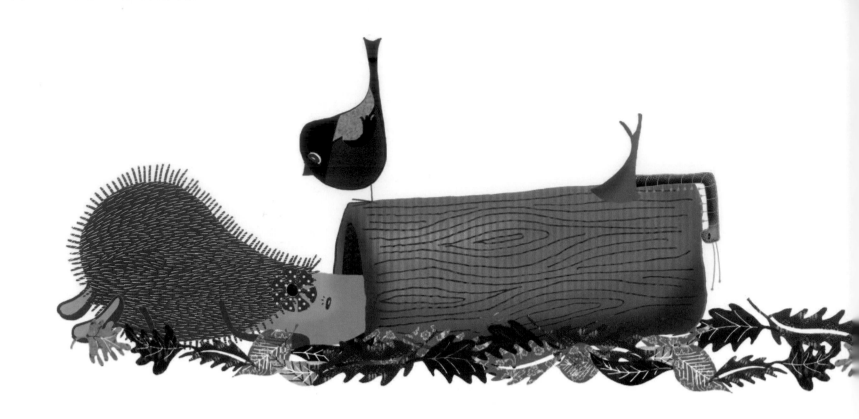

Hattie hunted.

The squeaky thing searched.

They looked... and looked...

Horace waited...and waited...until...

...SURPRISE!!!

Horace popped out of a pumpkin.

They squealed in fright and delight.

Then a whoosh of wind blew the last leaves and left the branches bare, and it was time for the squeaky thing to go back to his family. Hattie felt sad again.

Horace had an idea so he whispered

it to their new little friend.

Hooray! Hattie was happy!

The tree was complete with colour,
and alive with leaves and laughter
and lots of new squeaky friends!

The End

'Hedgehugs, Hide and Squeak'
An original concept by Lucy Tapper and Steve Wilson
© Lucy Tapper and Steve Wilson
Written by Lucy Tapper and Steve Wilson
Illustrated by Lucy Tapper

Published by MAVERICK ARTS PUBLISHING LTD
Studio 3A, City Business Centre, 6 Brighton Road, Horsham, West Sussex, RH13 5BB
© Maverick Arts Publishing Limited +44 (0)1403 256941

Published October 2016

A CIP catalogue record for this book is available at the British Library.

ISBN 978-1-84886-233-3

Maverick
arts publishing
www.maverickbooks.co.uk

Hedgehugs - Lovingly created by Lucy Tapper & Steve Wilson

Lucy Tapper is an illustrator, artist and designer. She loves all things beautiful and likes to surround herself with wild flowers, pretty fabrics and colour. Lucy is the creative force behind www.fromlucy.com.

Steve Wilson is Lucy's business partner at FromLucy and has a long history in children's TV presenting and writing music, hence his love of words, stories and characters.

Steve and Lucy live in a little cottage in Devon with their two daughters Daisy and Holly.

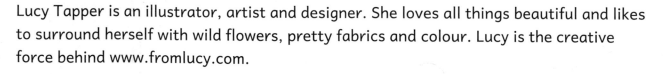